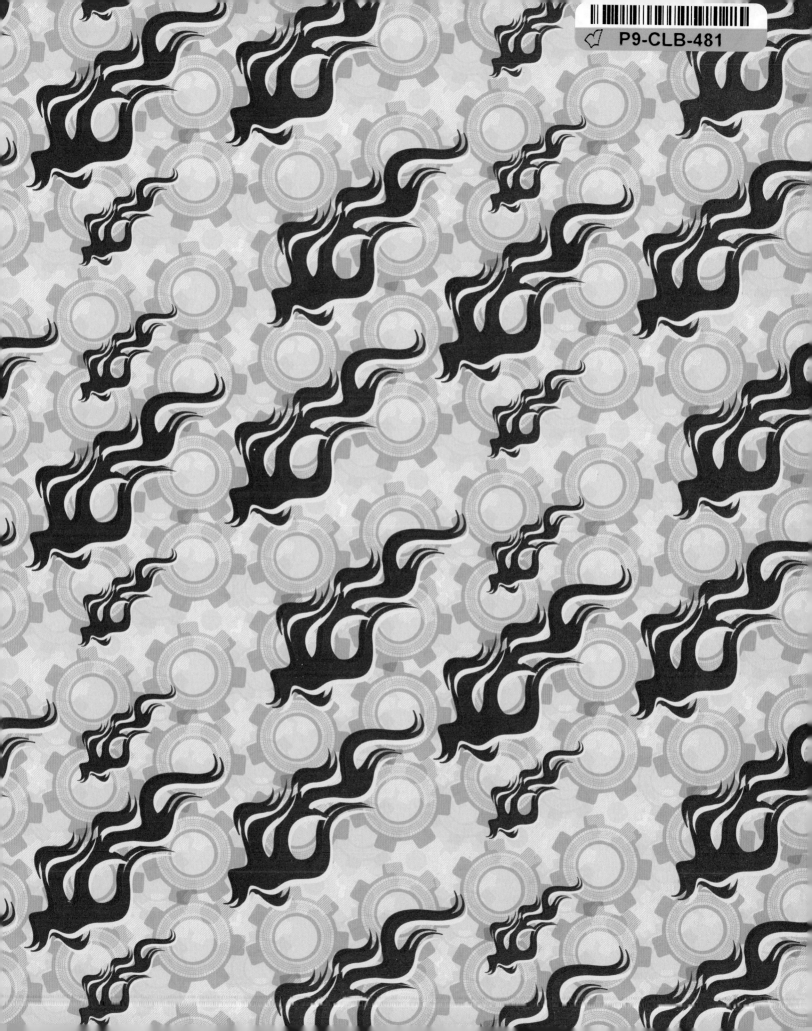

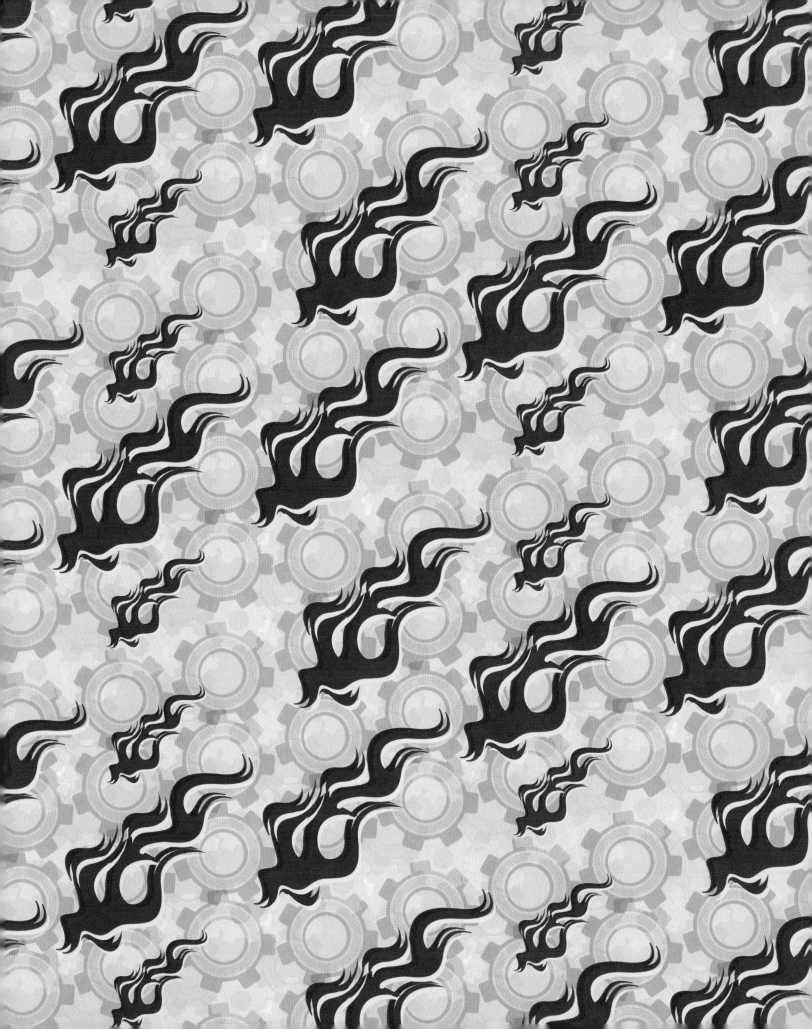

Adapted by Frank Berrios • Based on the teleplay "Blaze Christmas" by Jeff Borkin
Illustrated by Dynamo Limited

 A GOLDEN BOOK • NEW YORK

© 2016 Viacom International Inc. All rights reserved. Published in the United States by Golden Books, an imprint of Random House Children's Books, a division of Penguin Random House LLC, 1745 Broadway, New York, NY 10019, and in Canada by Penguin Random House Canada Limited, Toronto. Golden Books, A Golden Book, A Big Golden Book, the G colophon, and the distinctive gold spine are registered trademarks of Penguin Random House LLC. Nickelodeon, Blaze and the Monster Machines, and all related titles, logos, and characters are trademarks of Viacom International Inc.

randomhousekids.com

ISBN 978-0-399-55353-0

Printed in the United States of America

10 9 8 7 6 5 4 3 2 1

Random House Children's Books supports the First Amendment and celebrates the right to read.

'Twas the night before Christmas,
and all through Axle City,
big-wheeled Monster Machines
were making their homes look pretty.

Stripes put a wreath on his tree house,
and Starla decorated her barn.
Zeg got ready for Christmas
with ornaments, tinsel, and yarn.

Darington was so excited,
he jumped to his highest height!
Everyone knew they'd be getting
a visit from Santa tonight!

Meanwhile, Blaze and AJ
were far, far away,
helping Santa get ready
for another Christmas Day!

Blaze raced around the workshop as elf trucks tossed presents into Santa's magic bag.

"Santa's bag can hold presents for everyone in the world!" said AJ.

"My elves and I make sure we've got the perfect present for every boy and girl," said Santa. "Everyone should feel special on Christmas!"

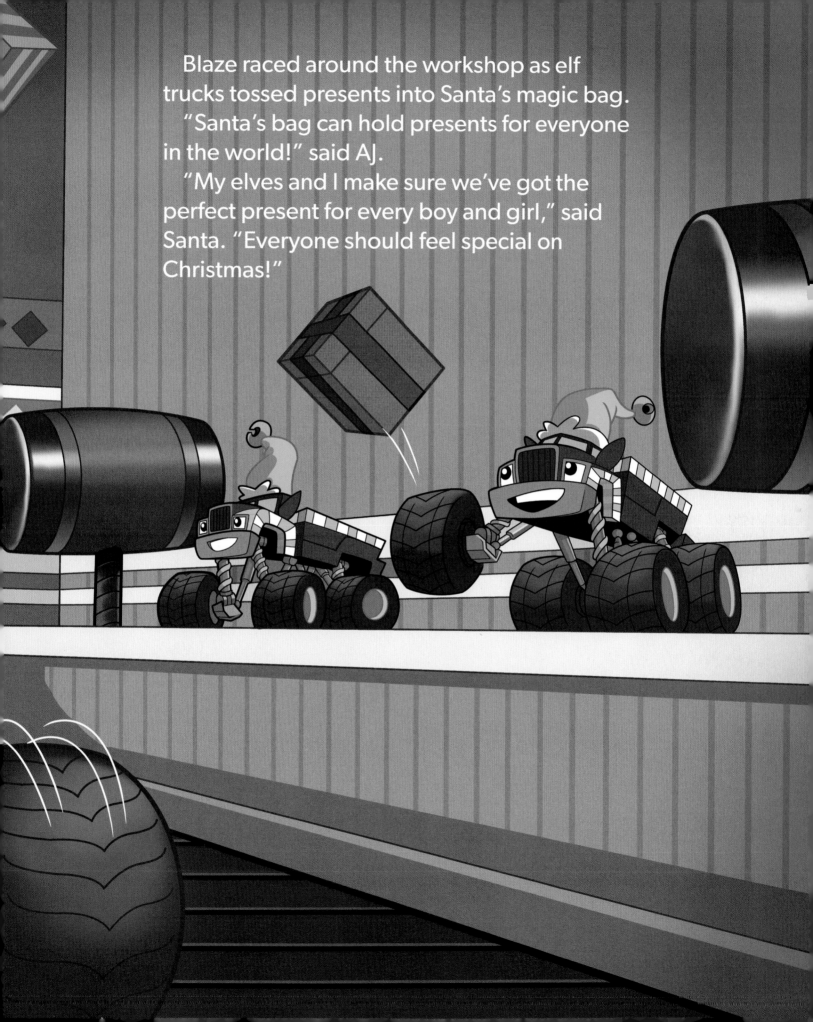

"The present meter says the bag is full!" exclaimed Blaze.

"Ho, ho, ho! Now I've got Christmas presents for everyone!" chuckled Santa Claus.

Santa and his friends were so busy that no one noticed two uninvited guests.

"Hey, Crusher, what are we doing in Santa's workshop?" asked Pickle.

"I want to look in Santa's bag and find *my* Christmas present," whispered Crusher. But before he could find his present, the bag began to roll away . . . with Crusher on top of it!

"Oh, no! The Christmas presents are getting away!" yelled an elf truck.

"Quick, after them!" said Blaze. He, AJ, and Santa raced after Crusher and the presents!

The bag rolled down a hill. It spilled open, and presents soared through the air in every direction!

"My magic bag is empty. Now I can't deliver my presents to anyone," Santa said sadly.

"Don't worry, Santa," said AJ. "Those presents are out there somewhere."

"And AJ and I are going to find them!" added Blaze.

"Wait—I want to come, too," begged Crusher.

"Good for you, Crusher! You feel bad, and now you want to help get all the presents back," said Pickle.

"*All* the presents? No way. I just want to get *my* present back," replied Crusher.

"Remember, Crusher, it's important that you help Blaze find *everyone's* present," said Santa. "Everyone should feel special on Christmas."

Blaze and Crusher raced off. Before long, they arrived at some ice-crystal caves.

"Hey, look up there!" said AJ. "A whole bunch of presents are frozen in the ice!"

Crusher tried to use a suction-cup bow and arrow to get the presents, but his toy arrow couldn't fly far enough to grab them.

Then Blaze had an idea. "Let's be engineers and build a *better* bow and arrow!" he said. "Engineers are scientists who figure out how to build new things."

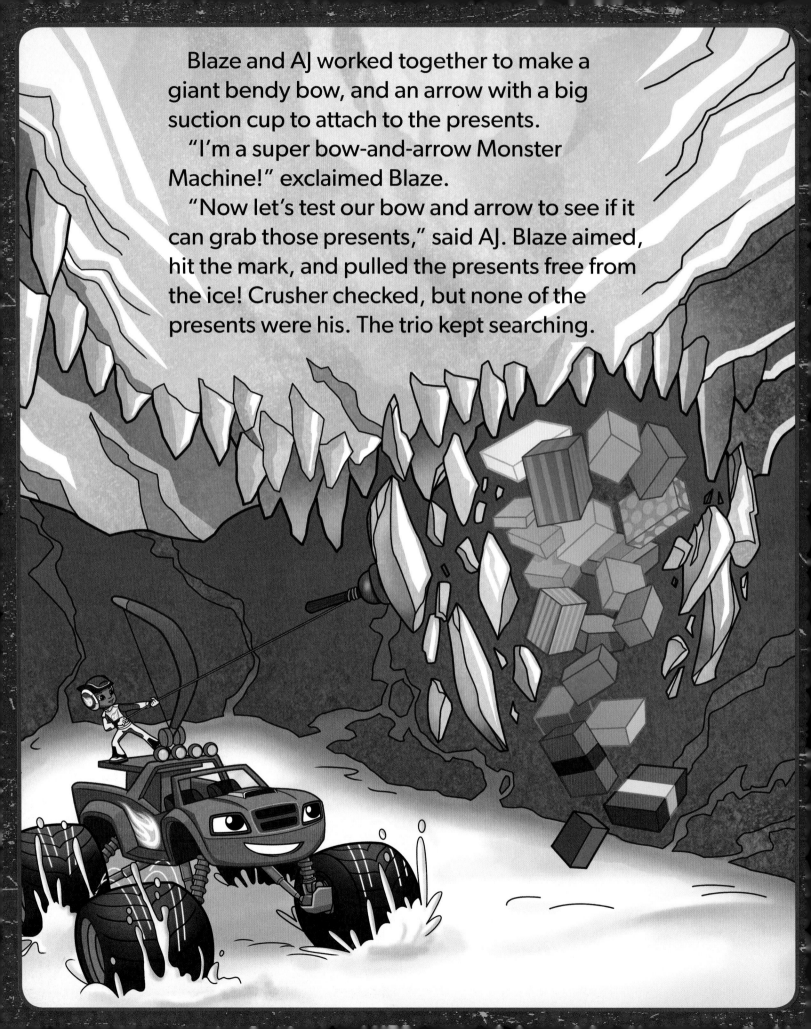

Blaze and AJ worked together to make a giant bendy bow, and an arrow with a big suction cup to attach to the presents.

"I'm a super bow-and-arrow Monster Machine!" exclaimed Blaze.

"Now let's test our bow and arrow to see if it can grab those presents," said AJ. Blaze aimed, hit the mark, and pulled the presents free from the ice! Crusher checked, but none of the presents were his. The trio kept searching.

Soon they spotted a pile of presents at the bottom of a very steep hill covered in candy canes!

"We have to make a sled that goes really fast!" said AJ. "Let's build a sled with a turbojet engine!"

"Woo-hoo! I'm a turbo-sled Monster Machine!" said Blaze. He took off with a burst down the candy-cane cliff and used his tow hook to snag the presents. Blaze added them to Santa's bag.

"Look! The red line on Santa's bag is going up!" noticed AJ. "That means we've found almost all the Christmas presents."

Crusher peered into the bag. "All these presents, and none of them are for me!" he whined.

The group continued.

They came to Snowball Mountain, which was shooting giant snowballs! To stop the snowballs, Blaze transformed into a big water blaster. "Oh, yeah! I'm a water-blastin' Monster Machine!" he shouted. "Time to get those Christmas presents."

When the Monster Machines reached the top of the
mountain, Crusher found what he was looking for.
    "I got my present!" he sang. But while the big blue
truck celebrated, the ice on the mountaintop began
to give way!
    "Oh, no! Santa's bag is falling!" cried AJ.
    "It's too heavy," said Blaze. "I can't pull it up
by myself."

"Well, good luck with that!" Crusher said. "I've already got my present." The present made him feel special. But then Crusher remembered what Santa had said: *everyone* should feel special on Christmas. "If those presents fall, no one will get a present from Santa. And then no one will feel special on Christmas! I've got to save those presents!"

Crusher went back to Blaze. Using their tow hooks, Blaze and Crusher worked together to save the Christmas presents.

Then Santa appeared!
"Look, Santa! We got all the presents!" said Crusher.
"That's wonderful," Santa replied. "Now we just
need some way to deliver them before it's too late."

"I can do it!" offered Blaze. "With Blazing Speed, I can help you deliver the presents super fast!"

"Ho, ho—that's it!" chuckled Santa. "Blaze, you can be my sleigh tonight!"

Blaze quickly transformed into a super sleigh.

"Let's deliver some Christmas presents!" said super-sleigh Blaze. AJ, Santa, and Crusher hopped aboard. With a burst of Blazing Speed, they took off into the night sky.

"Ho, ho, ho!" said Santa, and he held on tight.

And so it was, with Blaze as the sleigh,
Santa's gifts were delivered for Christmas Day.
And as they flew out of sight, we heard a phrase:
"Merry Christmas to all! And to all a 'Let's blaaaze!'"

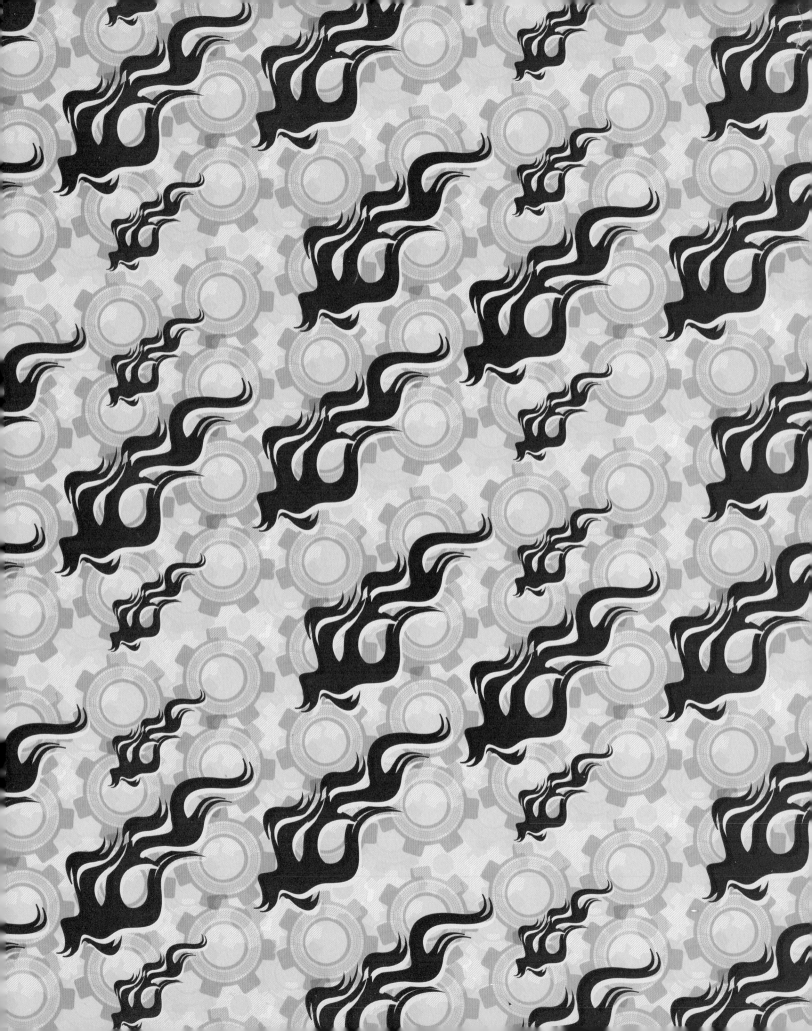